Rosie
Goes to School

Written by Susannah Bradley
Illustrated by Rebecca Archer

Hippo Books
Scholastic Children's Books
London

Scholastic Children's Books,
Scholastic Publications Ltd,
7-9 Pratt Street, London NW1 OAE, UK

Scholastic Inc.,
730 Broadway, New York, NY 10003, USA

Scholastic Canada Ltd,
123 Newkirk Road, Richmond Hill,
Ontario, Canada L4C 3G5

Ashton Scholastic Pty Ltd,
PO Box 579, Gosford, New South Wales,
Australia

Ashton Scholastic Ltd,
Private Bag 1, Penrose, Auckland,
New Zealand

First published by Scholastic Publications Ltd, 1992

Text copyright © 1992 by Susannah Bradley
Illustrations copyright © 1992 by Rebecca Archer

ISBN 0 590 55050 0

Printed in Spain by Mateu Cromo, Madrid

10 9 8 7 6 5 4 3 2 1

Rosie woke up early.
  "Today is special!" she told Freddy the cat.
"I'm going to school for the very first time!"

"Why do I have to go to school, Mum?"
asked Rosie. "You and Dad don't!"

   "No, but we did when we were children," said
Mum. "Going to school is fun. There are lots
of toys and books, and there will be games
to play."

"You will make new friends there, too," said Dad. "And you will become so clever! My goodness, school is going to make my Rosie very clever indeed."

"Oh, Dad!" said Rosie.

"What a lot of children!" said Rosie, when
Mum took her to school. "Are they all going
to school?"

"Yes," said Mum. "All children have to go to
school, as soon as they are old enough."

"Oh dear," said Rosie. "I won't know anybody."

Just then, Rosie's friend Laura ran up to her.
"Hello, Rosie!" she said. "I forgot you
would be starting school today, too! I hope
we can sit together."

"This is where you leave your coats and lunchboxes," said Laura's mum.

"Oh, yes," said Rosie's mum. "There is
Laura's peg – and here is yours, Rosie, with a
picture of a rabbit beside it."

"Mine has a lion," said Laura.

"I don't want you to go away," said Rosie.

"Don't worry," said Mum. "You'll have a lovely time, and I will be here at the end of the day to take you home for tea."

Rosie and Laura went into the classroom and sat down with the other children.

"Good morning, everyone," said the teacher. "My name is Miss Brown. Now, has everyone found somewhere to sit?"

One boy was still standing up.
  "Look, Tom, there's a seat next to Laura,"
said Miss Brown, kindly. "That can be your
place."
  Then Miss Brown read out everyone's
names from a big book called The Register.

"Please, Miss Brown, where is the toilet?"
asked Rosie.

"The toilets are through here," said Miss Brown. "You can use them whenever you like, and there are washbasins, too, for washing your hands afterwards."

At playtime, Miss Brown said that they could
go outside. But Tom didn't want to go.

"Come with us, Tom," said Rosie. "We're going to play ball."

After playtime Miss Brown said, "Now I'm going to read a story. Everyone must be quiet and listen."

Rosie liked the story. It was about a rabbit who went to school.

Then they did some drawing. There were lots
of crayons to use.

"What a lot of nice pictures!" said Miss Brown. "Your mummies will like to see these when they come to take you home."

Rosie had drawn Freddy the cat.
 "I wish I had a cat like Freddy at home,"
said Laura.

Just then, a bell rang. Miss Brown said it was lunchtime.

"I hope I have some nice sandwiches," thought Rosie.

They were cheese and tomato, Rosie's
favourite kind!
 "I've got cheese and tomato, too!"
giggled Laura.

In the afternoon, Miss Brown got out lots of toys.

"You can play with whatever you like," she said. "Or you can sit in the quiet corner and look at a book."

Rosie and Tom played in the sandbox, but
Laura went to the quiet corner with a book.

Later, Rosie did a jigsaw all by herself.

It was soon time to go home. Mum arrived to
meet Rosie.

"Did you have a good day?" asked Mum.
"It was fun," said Rosie. "Can I come again
tomorrow?"